CHAPTER THIRTEEN

CAN ONE LOVE ERASE ANOTHER?

VICTOR PAUL

Copyright © 2020 by Victor Paul

Follow Victor Paul on Instagram: instagram.com/victorpauldomain

First paperback edition November 2020

Cover design by Daniela Owergoor
Typeset by Post Pre-press Group, Brisbane

A catalogue record for this
book is available from the
National Library of Australia

NATIONAL
LIBRARY
OF AUSTRALIA

ISBN 978-0-6450135-0-4 (paperback)
ISBN 978-0-6450135-1-1 (ebook)

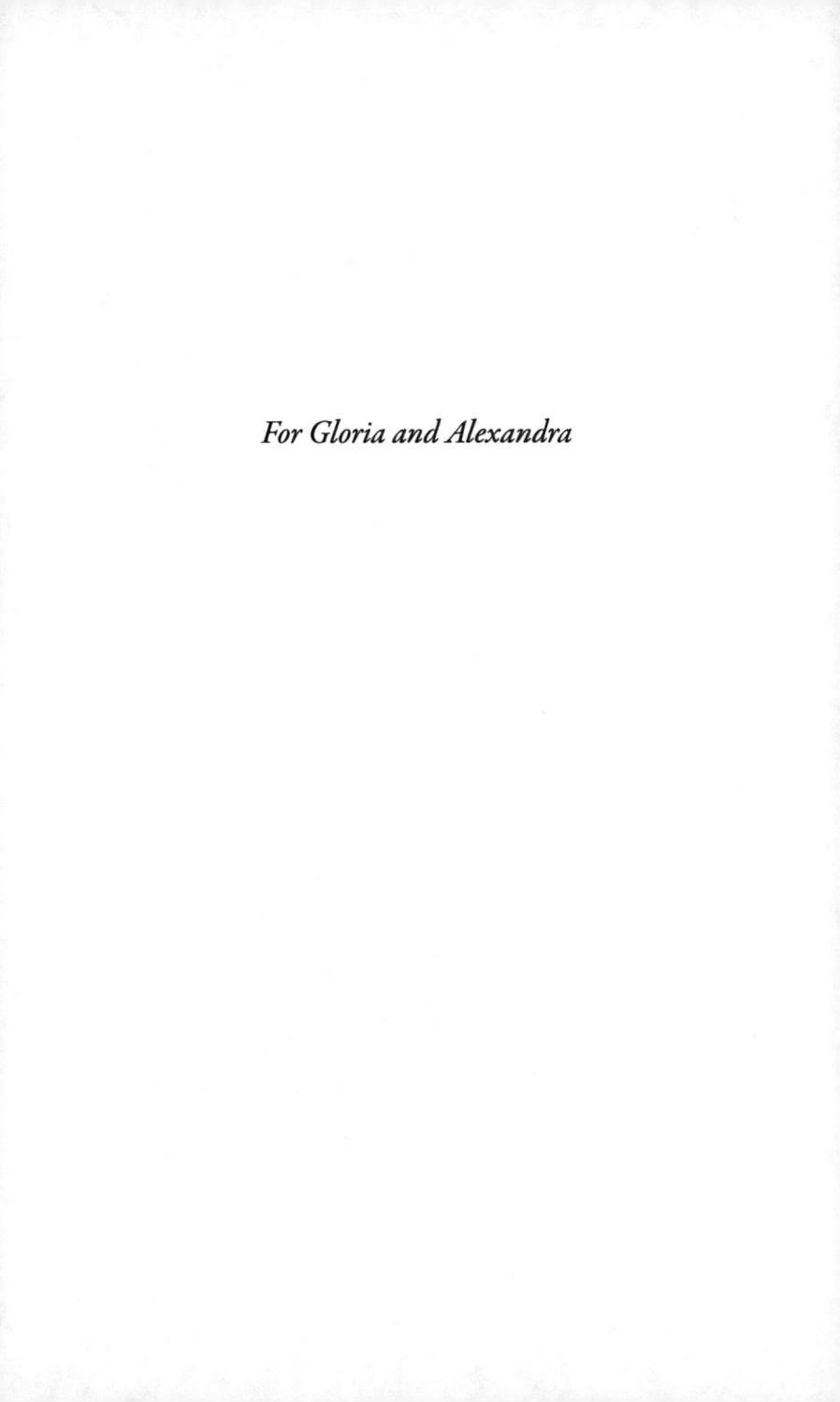

For Gloria and Alexandra

PROLOGUE

Pete's eyes roved over his sheet of paper. There was a drop of blood. He dropped his pen and looked at his hands. There was not an open wound in sight. The drop of blood spread out like the roots of a tree. A monstrous fear gripped him as he stood up from his desk and watched the roots expand. His mouth opened like a deep cave, but no sound emerged. He stretched out his hands to hold back unknown forces, his face a mask of horror. On the bloodied paper in black ink were the words *Chapter Thirteen*. A familiar woman's voice whispered into his ear. He woke up gasping for air, damp from trickles of ice-cold sweat. His nightmare was far from over.

CHAPTER 1

1981

Chapter thirteen found Pete sitting before a blank sheet of paper, unable to move any further past the events that had taken place ten years ago. The tip of his pen touched the paper, but his eyes stared blankly into space. It would be an exciting moment for most writers, reaching the conclusion, but this was not the case for Pete.

He snapped out of his daze and dropped his pen, covering his face with his hands. It almost seemed like an impossible task, writing chapter thirteen. He had failed to write the final chapter, even after many attempts; he didn't know where to start. The words just didn't seem to translate from thought to sentences.

Pete looked at the clear glass of water that sat on the table in his hotel room. It reminded him of the island of Marigua and its beautiful waters. Memories of the island started to flood his thoughts. His body could almost feel the heat of the island, just as he had first felt it when he arrived in Marigua in the summer of 1971.

His breathing started to get heavy and he stood up from his desk. Falling backwards onto the hotel's single bed, he covered his face with both hands. He felt paralysed by painful thoughts; guilty and angry with himself. Fear and anxiety began to grip him.

He had contemplated not writing his final book on so many occasions, but his fan base had been eagerly waiting and he knew it would be a huge let-down if he came this far and failed to complete it. Pete had promised his fans he would deliver a final book before he took a new job as a lecturer at Boston University. Naturally, his fans were upset, but he mentioned that it was something he needed to do—take a break from writing and move on to something different for a few years with the promise that he might one day write again.

Pete sat up. The table lamp illuminated the pen and paper that rested on the table with a ghostly silence. The events that had taken place on the island had been buried so long in his heart. He knew that it needed to be said and he felt that writing this novel would be the best way for him to reach some sort of closure. Maybe, it could even help him find peace.

He took a moment and closed his eyes. The sound of waves filled his ears. He could almost feel the wind blowing against his hair, as it had many years ago. He could taste the salt in the air. The vivid clear waters of Marigua engulfed his vision and he remembered how he had felt as the ship blew its horn, announcing it was ready to leave Boston. This clearly was no distant memory. Pete could feel the same emotions he had felt that very day. He was young, enthusiastic, hopeful and ambitious.

Pete opened his eyes. *Julia.* The name flashed across his mind as a painful reminder. He sometimes wished that he had never gone to that island then he never would have met her. His heart cried out her name; it always felt like a stab in his heart. Their lives had become intertwined for just two months, but the painful memories it had given him had lasted over a decade. It almost felt like yesterday. He wished that there was a way he could switch off his brain to those thoughts.

He stood up from his bed and walked towards the table. He looked at the words *Chapter Thirteen*. The sounds in his head grew louder and louder. The waves, the horn sounding at the dock for the ship to leave, the local people of Marigua talking, Julia's voice calling his name. They were all making their presence known, one after the other, pieces of a dramatic orchestra. He covered his head with his hands, wishing they would stop.

His body began screaming out for more air; his breathing got deeper and heavier. He took a long, hard look at the words and placed a full stop after the chapter number, then blacked out.

CHAPTER 2

Dark waters surrounded Pete. He noticed a familiar woman a distance away. Her lifeless body danced gently to the vibrations of the icy water. Her eyes were closed but her body was facing Pete, as if his gaze could bring her back to life. Her face was obscured by the strands of hair bouncing off her face to the gentle rhythm of the water. The pounding of Pete's heart was sending more and more vibrations across the water. As it got louder and louder, the gentle ballet dance of the woman changed into frantic arm movements, her hair thrown in random directions by the disturbance.

A gush of bright red water burst from the woman's body towards Pete. Pete took a deep breath and swam as fast as he could, away from the bloodied water that was snaking its way towards him. He didn't stop until he touched what felt like a metal pole, and in that instant, he felt the touch of thin bony fingers upon his shoulders.

'Oh God!' exclaimed Pete.

'Are you okay sir?' asked a young man with a concerned look on his face.

Pete came to his senses. It was a bright morning at his local pool and a young man in the pool was awaiting his answer. The lifeless woman had disappeared, and the water was nothing but a clear blue. The bloodied snake in the water had vanished. Pete slowly began to calm down.

'Sir?' said the young man again.

'Oh, I'm fine. It's just ...' said Pete, trying to string some words together.

The young man looked unsure.

'I'm fine,' said Pete again, giving him a weak smile as if to thank him for his concern. As the man nodded and walked away, Pete slowly climbed out of the pool.

Pete headed straight to his usual café. Over the years, he had found himself enjoying the noise of the café as much as peace and quiet when penning his books. He loved Boston—it was a place full of memories for him. Boston was the place where his Irish parents had started their life together when they first came to America. Pete's father was called to serve at the war front in 1944, and had never returned to see him born the following year.

'The usual, Pete?' asked the young waitress, Erin.

Erin was born in America but she was a very proud Irish woman who always made it a point to wear something green for the day. She had a lovely smile to greet everyone and had come to know Pete as a regular of the café and their local writing celebrity.

'Yes, the usual please.'

Pete smiled at Erin and took a seat at his usual spot near the end of the café beside a large window that overlooked the street. It was a spot where he could look out into the sky to feel the peace and tranquillity. He unzipped his bag, revealing a whole heap of sectioned papers. The last section had only one piece of paper. He pulled it out and placed it on the table, wondering if he would ever finish the chapter and release his final novel.

He wished the chapter would simply write itself— anything to spare him from this painful journey. The months of nightmares were not helping with the completion of the final chapter either.

'Coffee's here, Pete.'

'Oh. Thanks.'

He took a sip of his coffee, looking at the piece of paper. Then, with determination, he reached for the pen in his bag, his thoughts racing. His hands were desperately urging him to start the chapter, but his mind was preventing him from writing anything. It was like a war within him. He pressed the tip of the pen hard against the paper to write the first word then paused for a moment, as though refuelling his strength.

Then, disappointedly, he released the strong pressure against the paper and dropped his pen back into his bag. Chapter thirteen found its way into its section once again with nothing further written than the night before. He stood up and grabbed his bag, abandoning the single-sipped coffee on his table and leaving the café abruptly, defeated by the demons in his head.

CHAPTER 3

Pete hurried past the park and across the street, walking towards his apartment. Flashes of thoughts, like lightning bolts, struck him one after the other. The guilt was overwhelming and unbearable. He quickened his pace, as if the faster he walked the calmer he would feel. His heart raced as though it was meant to hit a higher beat with each passing moment. He started to feel lightheaded and the lights around him started to dim as if he was about to leave the world and enter another.

'Pete!' said a woman in a white floral dress.

Pete was thrown back into reality, startled by the sound of his name.

'Pete? Are you alright?'

A sense of relief flowed through him as he realised it was his wife, Marie. Speechlessness caught him for a brief second.

'God, you look like you've seen a ghost. Are you alright?'

'I'm fine. I was just ... heading back home. I just didn't have a good sleep last night at the hotel.'

'I thought you were going to be writing in the café for the next few hours?'

'I thought so too, but ...'

'Well, come home then. You look like you need some rest.'

'I'm sure I do. Here, let me help you with that stuff,' said Pete, taking some of the groceries off Marie.

Pete and Marie had been married for nine years. He had hidden years of guilt and anxiety from Marie by blaming any of his erratic behaviours on his writing career. He knew Marie had begun to accept that his career as a writer was not a regular job and it was the probable cause of his stressed nature.

He occasionally headed off to a hotel, checked himself in and came back with chapters of a book written, having forgone every potential moment of sleep through a highly caffeinated night. Marie had openly said to him that part of her looked forward to him taking on regular hours when he became a lecturer, hoping that it could bring him to some sort of normality.

As Pete opened the door into the apartment, he could sense Marie was itching to question him.

'Pete, did you manage to write anything at all?'

He wrestled with the right words, hesitant to tell Marie that he just couldn't write it. He knew he could be opening up a whole new chapter to his marriage and the thought of it scared him.

'I did write something, but it wasn't what I wanted and I had to scrap it. I'll come up with something after lunch.'

Marie smiled encouragingly, which gave Pete a gentle sense of relief. For years, he had forcefully pushed out thoughts of Marigua whenever they came to him. However, writing the final book was bringing him back to the very thoughts he had spent years escaping from. Strangely, he felt if he could just write the events of what happened as a fictional book, he might finally be free from the guilt.

'I'm going to head to the study to see if I can get anything at all written down or at least pen down some ideas while you prepare lunch.'

Marie smiled and waved him off.

He went into his study and sat back on his chair. He closed his eyes and imagined the drift of the waves as they pushed the ship towards Marigua. It truly was a remarkable island, surrounded by enchanting waters and amazing views, endless opportunities—and only three hours away from Boston, no less.

Sometimes, he wished he hadn't felt that way; maybe he wouldn't have boarded the ship to Marigua looking for something new. And yet, what happened on that island had strangely brought him to Marie in the end. There was no way of separating the events by any logical sense in his head.

As he closed his eyes and thought about how he was going to overcome the barriers of his final chapter, a spark flashed across his thoughts, like a lightbulb that had suddenly ignited. Pete realised where he could write the final chapter. He thought of the place and visualised it in his mind. He imagined himself sitting and writing.

'This is the place I'm going to write the final chapter,' he said to himself with sheer determination.

CHAPTER 4

1971, 10 years ago

The exotic island of Marigua was just a few hours away from the Port of Boston. It was where Americans went for a quick getaway—at least the wealthy ones. The locals of Marigua had become quite accustomed to American tourists. A few wealthy American business-men resided on the island, controlling some of the major businesses that were backed by rich American investors. The Americans controlled most of the port's business activities, more so than the local government itself.

Pete had decided to take a chance and travel to Marigua to find work and hopefully a new life. The emptiness he had felt in Boston after the death of his mother had pushed him towards new shores. He boarded a ship that was due to arrive in Marigua in the afternoon. The calm waters of the Port of Boston and the singing of birds welcoming the morning all seemed to reassure Pete that he was making the right decision. The night before, he had almost decided not to go ahead with his plan, but nothing—and no one—appeared to offer a strong reason for the single twenty-six-year-old man to stay; he was alone. So, he packed his bag, promising himself that he was going to board that ship to Marigua and make a new life for himself.

'You can't wait to get there can you?' said a man who seemed to be about the same age as Pete.

'What makes you say that?'

'You were staring straight in the direction of the island for a long time.'

Pete chuckled. 'I've heard so much about Marigua and I want to see it for myself.'

'Steve,' said the man, extending his hand.

'Pete.'

'You don't look like you're going for a holiday Pete,' said Steve as he looked towards a group of well-dressed Americans.

'Is it that obvious? No, I'm not. I am going to look for work in Marigua.'

'Do you know someone there?'

'I wouldn't say so, but a friend of my mother's told

me an Irish businessman from Boston has opened a pub and restaurant; I'm hoping he might give me a job.'

'So you left your mum in Boston to go to Marigua for work?'

'She actually passed away a few months ago,' said Pete.

There was a silence in the air for a moment.

'Oh, God bless her soul. Sorry, Pete.'

'That's okay. We all have our stories—that's why we're on this ship I suppose. What about you? Why are you going to Marigua?'

'Me? Both my parents died in the war. I worked as a labourer in Boston. I heard they were trying to build a cathedral in Marigua and need some labourers to get the job done. So that's where I am heading.'

Pete looked at Steve earnestly. 'Well, let's hope that this journey to Marigua changes our lives then.'

'Hope so!'

Both men went silent and stared into the endless horizon, waiting for the outline of the island to appear as the ship began its journey.

CHAPTER 5

1981

As Marie prepared lunch,she remembered the first time she'd set eyes on Pete. When he had first walked into the publishing house she was working for at that time, looking for the owner and chief editor—she'd been instantly attracted to him. He was handsome, with eyes that were deep and beautiful. Marie had no idea at that time that Pete was going to be working for John; her heart had skipped with excitement when she'd found out.

As the months drifted by, she was more and more drawn to his charming manners and good looks. She started to find ways to get close to him at work. Finally, after months of hints and making him numerous cups of coffee on the pretext that she was going to make herself one anyway, Pete got the hint and asked her out. He'd seemed mysterious to her at times, but she loved that he was genuine and well mannered.

Marie had many nights of laughter and fun with Pete. She seemed to be able to talk about almost anything with him. The nights usually ended with Marie giving him a kiss on the cheek and heading back alone to her apartment.

After three months of dinner dates and movie nights out, she had finally held Pete's hand for the first time.

.....

1972, nine years ago
Marie opened the door to her apartment. A nervous feeling tingled its way through her body. A small thought flashed in her mind—had she invited him over too soon? Her conservative upbringing made her a little uneasy with a man in her apartment at this time of the night. Her heart pumped with strong feelings, addressing those questions as Pete entered the apartment. She felt comfortable with him and her decision.

'These paintings are beautiful. Wow!'

'Do you like them?'

'Like them? They are absolutely amazing. Are these all yours?'

Marie felt the blood pumping straight into her cheeks. The paintings were close to her heart and she enjoyed every minute of her free time working on her artwork. She had been working in the publishing house, but what she truly adored were her paintings. She had never shown them to anyone until now.

'Yes, they are. It's just a hobby.'

'You truly are a wonderful artist. A woman of many talents, I have to say!'

Marie could feel the rays of admiration hit her. She could see Pete's eyes wandering across her face, eyes and lips. Feeling a little embarrassed, she directed him to her latest unfinished work.

'It's going to be a painting of the local dock; I'm thinking of having a person in the foreground.'

'Do you have a person in mind?'

Marie pondered for a second and an idea flashed brightly as her face lit up.

'I do now!' she said with a cheeky smile.

She took Pete's hands and directed him to stand behind her paint-marked easel.

'Don't move and stay still.'

'Am I going to be the person in your painting?'

'Shhh.'

As Marie took her brush and started to paint the outline of Pete's face, a shadow cast over her. A warm hand touched her face and she found Pete's eyes looking into hers. A warm kiss brushed her lips and she kissed him back. She dropped her paintbrush and pulled him closer, kissing him passionately.

Their clothes soon found the ground next to the paintbrush. It was a night Marie never forgot.

CHAPTER 6

1971, 10 years ago

The ship sounded its loud horn to make its presence known to the port of Marigua. Pete could see the port bustling with people and activity. People swarmed around the colourful food stalls. In the distance, a police officer was preparing his checkpoint crew for the arriving tourists. Pete could feel the excitement bursting inside him. He quickly made his way to the front, as if it were a race. The feeling within him was so intense that he could hardly keep his feet from tapping away as he waited to disembark. It was as if fast-paced jazz music was playing in his head and his body was tapping and moving to multiple rhythms.

The ship came to a stop, shaking from side to side as the strong waves pushed against it. Pete saw Steve a few metres away, sandwiched between everyone as he prepared to disembark.

'Good luck Pete!' shouted Steve.

Pete nodded and shouted back, 'You too!'

Pete got to the immigration checkpoint, where an officer with a stern look and a demanding voice barked, 'Passport!'

Pete's feet were still tapping with eagerness. The immigration officer eyed him suspiciously. He reached into his pocket and handed his passport over as if his entire life depended on his entry into Marigua. He needed immigration to believe that he was just an American tourist.

Mariguan laws strictly forbade Americans from coming onto the island for work. The law did, however, permit Americans who started and owned businesses to live and work in Marigua. Despite this, with the correct amount of money and influence, many Americans who had come to Marigua had found a way to live on the island. Pete was hoping for the same.

'The reason for your visit?'

'Oh, just travel ... holiday ... a vacation!' said Pete with nervous laughter.

The immigration officer glanced to his left at a fellow officer and said something in the local language. Pete only caught the word *American* being uttered throughout the exchange.

The immigration officer looked at Pete again with a piercing eye, as if to uncover his real reason for coming to Marigua, but to Pete's delight, he stamped his passport, handed it back to him and shouted, 'Next!'

Pete exited the immigration gates and exhaled a sigh of relief. He was finally on the island; his journey had begun. Seconds later, a taxi driver rushed to him and got his attention.

'Do you need a Toko?' he asked, gesturing towards a three-wheeled vehicle.

'Where's the steakhouse at?' asked Pete.

The locals in Marigua who dealt with tourists could understand basic English. The influx of American tourism had clearly had an effect on the locals, who spoke a Mariguan language which was closely related to Spanish and Portuguese.

'Oh! The steakhouse? I'll take you to the steakhouse,' the taxi driver exclaimed with a big smile across his face. He placed his hands behind Pete's back as if to gently push him towards his taxi.

'No that's fine. I just want to know where it is.'

The taxi driver's smile vanished; he pointed briefly before dropping his hand, shaking his head at the other drivers to indicate that Pete had wasted his time and they were not going to get any business out of him. He had soon moved to the next tourist, offering the same big smile he had given Pete only seconds earlier.

Pete started to walk in the direction of the steakhouse. Tokos whizzed past him, one after the other, loaded with tourists. He adjusted the bag that was slung across his shoulder and started to walk as fast as he could, as if he was competing with the passing taxis.

He walked past several pubs and restaurants along the port and was tempted to go in and ask for work. However, he knew that the owner of the steakhouse was from Boston and that the association might help him get a job.

The streets were busy, bustling with people and noise. He walked past several tourists who were having their afternoon beer in the beach restaurants and pubs. However, the thoughts in Pete's head were dramatically louder than any noise in the street. He wondered if he would find the new life that he so desperately wanted on the island. He wandered along happily, smiling to himself at the snippets of conversation he heard along the way.

Pete reached the corner of the street. He looked up at the signboard and found himself looking into a large pub filled with people. He felt the heat under his skin being cooled off by the coastal wind. His life was just about to start!

CHAPTER 7

Pete headed straight for the entrance of the steakhouse. A young waiter greeted him as he was entering the restaurant.

'May I help you, sir?'

'I'm looking to speak with the owner,' Pete said as he looked into the restaurant.

The restaurant had a large bar filled with people. There were several tables set up outside, facing the beach. The ocean breeze blew freely in and out of the restaurant.

'The owner is out back, in the kitchen. What is it regarding?' asked the waiter.

'I'm looking for a job and was wondering if I could speak to the owner about it.'

The waiter paused for a moment before replying. 'Just wait here for a moment. I'll go see if I can get him for you.'

The waiter left Pete at the entrance and headed straight for the back of the kitchen.

The waiter came back. 'Derrick wants you to come to the kitchen to meet him.'

Pete followed the waiter to the end of the restaurant where the kitchen was. He could hear a man's laughter getting louder as they approached, even through the afternoon crowd of tourists eating and drinking. As the waiter pushed the door into the kitchen, Pete glimpsed a fat man with black back-combed hair laughing loudly with what appeared to be the chef.

The laughter stopped momentarily as both men looked at Pete.

'Derrick, this is the man who is looking for a job.'

'Yeah okay, leave us and we'll have a chat,' said Derrick.

The waiter left the kitchen in an instant.

'I'm here for—' started Pete.

'What sort of work are you looking for?

'Err … Anything really.'

'I got the best chef here already, so I definitely don't need a chef. Whereabouts in America are you from? Your accent sounds familiar.'

'I'm from Boston.'

'Ah, Boston! No wonder it sounded familiar. A boy from my hometown. It's been a while since I've been back.'

The anticipation broke a trickle of sweat down the side of Pete's forehead. His hand tapped the side of his thigh as he waited for Derrick's answer.

'Look lad, if you really just want any job, I am in need of a waiter who speaks English. Some of my American customers are getting annoyed speaking to the local waiters. The place is busy during lunch and dinner and I could use an extra hand. If you're interested, you can start today.'

'Sir, I would very much like to—'

'Call me Derrick. Let Thomas, who you met in the front, know that I've hired you; he'll show you around.'

'Thank you so much Derrick!'

Pete's heart jumped with excitement. He turned to rush out of the kitchen, but a question from Derrick brought him to an abrupt stop.

'Wait! Where you holding up, lad? Do you have a place to stay?'

Pete did not have an answer. He had hardly thought about it. He had put a lot of thought into getting onto the island and finding work, but as for somewhere to live, up until now, he had somehow believed that if he got the job, the rest would fall gracefully into place.

'Tell Thomas you need a place to stay. He'll let you know where to go. Most of the waiters stay at a place not too far from here. The accommodation is cheap. Basic stuff, you know.'

Pete felt like it was almost a blessing to have come to the steakhouse first, looking for a job. He had not only got a job that afternoon but found a place to stay.

'Thank you, Derrick.'

'Alright, don't take too long. It will get busier soon and I need Thomas to run the waiter crew instead of showing you around. I've got a business to run, so Godspeed.'

'I'll go see Thomas!'

Pete hurried to the front of the restaurant.

'Thomas?'

'Yes? You got the job?'

'Derrick said I can start work today. He asked if you'd show me around. I'm Pete, by the way.'

'Follow me and we will get you your uniform.'

As Pete followed Thomas into the storage room, Thomas explained that Derrick was a good boss as long as everyone did their job, kept the customers in the restaurant happy and did not spill any food or drink on the customers.

'You don't want to see Derrick angry,' warned Thomas, handing Pete his uniform.

'Derrick told me that you could show me where most of the staff stay.'

'Yeah, you can get cheap accommodation. Go to the left of the restaurant and look for the sign that says *Bovo Motel*. Go get changed—and be here soon, this place is going to get busier.'

A Mariguan woman with a flower in her hair greeted Pete at the motel reception. Pete handed her what it cost for a week, trying not to let it show on his face that he was now penniless. Everything seemed to be happening so fast. It seemed like only a minute ago he was at the port waiting to enter the island, and now he was already about to start his new job.

The woman showed Pete to his room. It had a small bed and reeked of cigarettes. The sheetless mattress had stains on it and the wardrobe was made of a few planks of cheap wood. There was a communal toilet that was shared between the rooms on his floor. The woman handed Pete the keys and reminded him that rent needed to be paid at the beginning of every week.

Pete hurriedly changed into his uniform and locked the room door behind him. The room was far from the island life that he had imagined. He quickened his pace as he headed to the restaurant. He promised himself that he would make his life better than what it was at this moment.

CHAPTER 8

1972, nine years ago

Pete held Marie's hand like he never wanted to let it go. In his right pocket, secretly tucked away, was a box which contained an ornament that would express how he truly felt about Marie after almost a year of courtship. His hand was starting to slide off Marie's with the nervousness he was feeling. He released Marie's hand and wondered how to put the words together or even start to articulate his intentions.

'Why are we at the dock this time of the night?'

'Erm ... I heard it is going to be a starry night and I wanted to see the stars with you.'

'Pete, there are no—'

Pete dropped to one knee and found himself looking up at Marie, whose expression was shifting between confusion and emotion. In one hand, he held a small opened red velvet box with a diamond ring in it.

'We complete each other's sentences all the time and I thought you would want to do that with me for the rest of your life.'

'Pete!'

'You are the most amazing woman I have ever met in my life. Will you marry me Marie?'

Pete waited anxiously for Marie's answer. He wondered for a brief moment if he had asked her too soon. However, the connection he felt with Marie was so intense that he knew she was the one for him. They had not spent a day without seeing each other since the night Marie had invited him over.

The chemistry between them was so blatantly visible that most people who met them had often mistaken them at first for a married couple. Pete used to laugh at how people had already married them even before it had happened.

He had inspired her to pursue her artwork, which led to her leaving the publishing firm and embarking on an artistic career that had recently started to take off. He loved that she encouraged him through his writing passion and he knew she loved him for the person he was. He loved Marie for everything she was and knew if there was one person in his life that he was going to call his wife, it would be Marie.

'Yes! Yes, I'll marry you!'

CHAPTER 9

1981

Pete could hear from a distance the sound of calm waves, gentle and musical to his ears. The sound grew louder as they generated momentum. As if a music conductor was present to instruct the waves, they began to make all sorts of violent sounds, growing stronger. The sounds got louder and louder and Pete began to feel breathless. He was drowning. The calm waves had suddenly turned violent and were on the path to kill him.

He felt the cold waters around him and there was not a soul around to call for help. Everyone must have drowned in the violent waves that swarmed the island. The beautiful waters of Marigua were now a deadly pit waiting to end his life. He could not even cry out to God for help—the water was entering his mouth, he was choking.

'Pete? Are you alright in there? Lunch is ready.'

A familiar voice brought Pete to semi-consciousness, leaving him puzzled as to which world was the real world. He knew he was surely drowning in the seas of Marigua; he could feel the coldness of the Atlantic waters and the ruthless waves crashing onto him one after another, drowning him and his guilt.

He saw a huge wave build up, about to swallow him, and just as his vision was obscured by the monstrous wave, a touch on his shoulder jolted him into full awareness.

'Pete! Are you alright?'

Pete looked at Marie, who was obviously waiting for an answer from him. He felt jumpy—on edge. Pete dismissed the question with a sweeping motion across his tired eyes.

'Just a bad dream, nothing much.'

The lunch table was so quiet that Pete could literally hear each and every sound that their knives and forks made against their plates. He could sense Marie was about to unload an uneasy question onto him and was not looking forward to it.

'How's the book coming along?'

'I have the last chapter to write and then it should be done. I'll finish it tomorrow.'

'Are you still sure about taking that job at the university?

'I am sure, Marie. Which is why I would really like to finish off writing my final book.'

The conversation on the book ended abruptly. Pete wondered if the day would ever come where he could share with Marie his deepest demons.

.....

The day had almost come to an end. Pete gave Marie a sombre goodnight kiss on the cheek. The darkness of his closed eyes was suddenly filled with colours from the scene of the first night he met Julia. The very thought of her name felt like a tonne of weight weighing down his heart.

Pete remembered the night she had come into the restaurant by herself. When he went to her table to serve her, she had an aura of strength around her. Her shoulders were thrown back confidently and a magnetic wave of beauty embraced her face at every angle. Her voice was honey, and the very words from her mouth were pure sweetness.

.....

1971, 10 years ago
'You're not expecting anyone?'

'Not tonight. I'll be having dinner on my own. Bring me the best wine you have on the menu.'

Pete came back to Julia's table with the most expensive bottle of wine. He carefully placed her glass down and began to pour some wine into it. He could feel Julia's eyes lock onto him.

'So you're the waiter that Monica has asked to look after me tonight?'

'That's right. If you need anything ma'am please let me know.'

'You can call me Julia. What's your name?'

'I'm Pete.'

'I didn't know Monica had an American waiter.'

'I'm new here.'

'What brought you here to Marigua?' asked Julia as she took a sip of wine.

'I needed a change.'

'Sometimes we all need a change.'

Pete wondered for a split second what had happened in Julia's life to make her sound the way she did. She intrigued him. He felt lucky at that point that Monica had told him to look after her for the night. He took every opportunity to talk to her on the pretext of serving her or asking her if everything was alright.

'Is there anything else I can get you, Julia?

'I'm fine for now. You sure are looking after me well tonight. I'll let Monica know.' said Julia with an appreciative smile.

As Pete cleared the last of the tables, he noticed Julia looking far off into horizons of the island. The restaurant, which sat on the corner of the street, had a perfect view of the ocean and the surrounding beach. He noticed that the bottle of wine on Julia's table was empty.

'We're closing now, Julia. Do you want some water?'

'You are handsome,' said Julia with a cheeky laugh, a little tipsy.

Pete felt slightly embarrassed.

'Pete! Close the place up now! Don't you want to go home?' shouted a voice from the kitchen.

'I feel like taking a walk along the beach. You want to join me?' asked Julia with a smile.

'Oh ... I ... um ... sure. I'm just about to finish, so yeah, if you could wait for me ... I'll—'

Julia grabbed her handbag, leaving a wad of cash to pay for the meal.

'I'll be just outside.'

Pete could not wait to see Julia. He rushed to the back of the restaurant to find her. She was smoking a Virginia Slim cigarette just in front of the restaurant and his heart was delighted to see her. He hesitated before asking her a question.

'You sure you don't want to go home Julia? You seem a little ...'

'We can take a walk over there,' she said, pointing

to the beachfront as she grasped his hand and started walking, completely ignoring Pete's comment.

'You know why I like walking on the beach Pete?'

'Why?'

'It makes me feel free. That's the feeling I get when I walk along the beach here. I was with someone for four years and I never felt free until I left him. He wants me to go back to him, but I've already booked a ticket back to America in a few weeks' time.'

'You're leaving Marigua for good?'

Pete's heart almost sank into the very ocean he was walking beside. He didn't want the night to end and he certainly didn't want the meeting of Julia to come to nothing. He wanted to know more about her. She had a strange magnetic effect that drew him to her. It was powerful and inexplicable.

'Yeah, I'm leaving Marigua for good. I need a change. I need to be back home—away from all this.' She laughed, 'I don't know why I'm telling you all this ... I've just met you.'

'I left Boston to have a change; that's why I came here. I don't really have anyone back home.'

'What about your family?'

Pete paused for a moment.

'My mum passed away a few months ago and my dad ... yeah...he isn't alive either. He died in the war.'

'I'm sorry to hear that. Doesn't it feel good when someone just listens to you? I mean, like, really listens to what you have to say, let's you speak and be heard.'

'I like listening to you speak,' said Pete with a smile.

Julia stopped walking at that moment, as if Pete had said something she had not heard in a very long time. It was almost as if forces of nature were throwing every magnetic field around them to join the two of them together.

'Three years ago, I left Boston to come here and work for Jason.'

'What were you doing before then?'

'I was working as a waitress.'

Julia paused for a moment, lost in thought.

'I'd like to know more about you, Julia.'

'I'm leaving in two months' time.'

Pete took in a deep breath and let the full effect of Julia spill right over him.

'Then I want to know everything about you in the next two months.'

Julia moved closer to Pete, touched his face and kissed him on the cheek. 'Pete, I really like you, I really do.'

CHAPTER 10

1981

Pete's feet hurried to take him to where he needed to be to write the final chapter. He could feel the surge of energy within him. The bag which hung over his shoulder bounced in all directions as he hurried through the fallen leaves. His body cut through each breeze that blew against him.

Pete wished a time machine could portal him to his destination in that instant. The moment to write chapter thirteen had finally come and he was going to seize it. As he got closer to his destination, he could see the beautiful horizon of sky-blue paint itself across the port.

As he approached the jetty, he could feel the mild breeze of the morning which had created mini hill-like structures across the sea surface. He walked to the end of the jetty and sat down, his mind fixated on the task ahead. Flocks of birds flew freely and yet in synchronised motions, performing ballet in the air.

Pete unzipped his bag and flipped through to a tab that read *Chapter Thirteen*, retrieving a single piece of paper. He looked at the only words written on it. He finally felt ready to write the last chapter. Facing the port waters and the horizon, he started writing.

The soft sounds of water crashing against the jetty and small waves against each other created an ambience, beckoning the memories that began to flow into Pete's head. As they flooded in one after the other, his pen performed its work, page after page. Time went by as words and paragraphs flowed: first one, then another, then another.

As the sun began to make its first descent into sunset, Pete found himself writing the very last sentence of the final chapter. The flock of birds had flown back to their home as the port watched the final light of the day fade. Chapter thirteen had finally been written.

CHAPTER 11

Pete arrived home with an expression of accomplishment written all over his face.

'You did it!'

'Yes. I finally did it. The final chapter has been written.'

'We must celebrate tonight.'

Pete felt like a needle had pricked him, reminding him of a painful memory. He had heard those very words before. His thoughts briefly floated into a sea of past memories; the image of a woman began to take form in his mind.

'Pete, are you okay?'

'Oh sorry, I was just thinking ...'

Pete's expression of joy and relief at successfully

writing the final chapter was replaced by a distant, lost expression.

'Well, I'll need to contact John and let him know that I've finished writing the book.'

'Pete, let's worry about that tomorrow. It's almost dinner time anyway. Let's head out to celebrate.'

Pete could see how excited Marie was for him, that she wanted to share his happiness.

'Alright, let's head out for dinner to celebrate. You pick the place; I'm too exhausted to decide.'

'Not a problem! You just get yourself ready and I'll make the reservations. You're going to love this place, Pete.'

....

Pete smiled at Marie to thank her for organising the small celebration. He pulled up at the parking lot facing a restaurant with a sign that he hadn't yet taken note of. He was more relieved than happy to know that he had finally written the book. He was hoping that he could finally feel free from the cage of guilt and pain that had imprisoned him for years.

As they walked towards the restaurant, the huge sign caught Pete's eye.

'Are we going to that steakhouse over there?' he asked.

'Yes! A girlfriend of mine recommended it and I thought since we haven't been here before we should give it a try.'

Pete could not help it; thoughts of Marigua drifted into his mind. He desperately fought any further thoughts or recollections, but they were stealing moments from him.

He had finished writing the book and there was so much to celebrate, but he seemed troubled. He was battling thoughts in his head.

'You can talk to me, Pete, if something is bothering you. Is it the new role at the university?'

Pete felt the urgent need to leap into the current world, away from his thoughts, to answer Marie's question. He could feel her discomfort. It was almost as though things were about to uncover themselves on their own somehow; his behaviour was clearly giving away that something was not right.

'I'm fine, Marie. Let's have a nice celebration. I'm glad to take the role at the university. It gives me a break from writing. I think I'm just overwhelmed.'

'Well, you'll need to just relax and enjoy the night then.'

Pete pulled Marie closer to him and felt her warmth as she wrapped her arm around his waist and they continued walking towards the restaurant. He did not want to ruin the happy moment, so he pushed the thoughts of Marigua forcefully out of his head. It did not seem to be the right time to talk to her about what had happened on the island. He chose to leave it for another day, just as he had done for the last ten years.

CHAPTER 12

1971, 10 years ago

'Come back with me to America,' whispered Julia as they lay naked in bed.

'You're asking a man to live with you after knowing him for a month?'

'Yes, I am asking a naked man in my bed after knowing me for over a month to live with me. *Yes* is the answer,' laughed Julia cheekily.

Pete pulled Julia closer to him and kissed her. As strong a woman as she was, there were moments of her girly behaviour that Pete adored. Her question silenced Pete, leaving his thoughts swinging like a pendulum. After all, he had barely started his new life in Marigua. He wanted to make something out of his life on the island and going back to Boston somehow represented a failure on his part. Another part of him embraced the new love he had found; it felt so right being with Julia, and starting a new life with her seemed exciting.

'We can both start a life together and give it a try. It doesn't have to just be a fling.'

'Why would you think it would just be a fling?' Pete sounded a little annoyed that Julia would think all they had was something casual in nature.

There was a brief pause; neither of them knew what to say. Pete could feel the words bursting out of his chest.

'I love ...'

He caught all of Julia's attention and a smile started to break out across her face.

'What I was going to say was that I care deeply about you. I mean, I have deep feelings for you—'

'Come on, say it ... *say it!*' she laughed.

Pete looked her in the eyes and wrapped his palm around her cheek. Then he said what he could no longer contain.

'I love you Julia!'

Pete saw Julia's smile disappear. A tear started to form in her eye. It fell silently upon her cheek. Pete felt her hugging him tightly like she never wanted to let him go.

CHAPTER 13

Julia could taste her own blood as her body was flung to the ground by a thundering slap from Jason's heavy hand. It echoed in the warehouse of the dock as a grim warning. The seagulls squawking in the background flew away, startled.

'Women! They want to know everything,' said Gus with a whisky-laden voice as he shook his head from side to side.

Gustavo, or Gus, as he usually went by, was a local Mariguan port superintendent who had a stern face with a thick moustache that sat angrily on his face. Julia had never been anywhere near comfortable around Gus. For years, she had never asked Jason about his dealings with him. All she knew was that he came once a month to the warehouse and collected two boxes of goods from America that Jason set aside for him.

However, as the years went on, she had noticed that Gus and Jason held conversations in whispers, and there were always two boxes specifically reserved for Gus. The boxes, as she began to notice, were always marked by a small piece of black tape. The burning question, which had started out as a small spark, gradually grew into explosive flames.

It was three years before Julia had finally summoned the courage to ask Jason what was in those boxes. The answer she received was a reflection of the state of her relationship with Jason. She worked for Jason and was to sign off on items arriving from America—mostly food items of all sorts to be delivered to the many flourishing restaurants on the island. Jason paid her for her work, but she was obviously not to question him about anything that took place at the warehouse.

Julia struggled to get back onto her feet, paralysed by shock and fear. Her bell-bottom jeans were stained by a puddle of oil that lay on the dusty warehouse floor. Blood was starting to ooze from a small cut on one of her elbows. Gus walked past her to pick up his boxes, not saying anything further as he exited the warehouse. She could hear Jason breathing heavily and was terrified to even look at him. As she began to sob, rooted firmly to the ground, Jason stormed out of the warehouse.

It was the first time she had been hit by Jason, but somehow she knew it wouldn't be the last.

CHAPTER 14

Julia sat uncomfortably on the Italian leather sofa waiting for Jason to come back. She had so many questions running in her head and spent the whole afternoon wondering where to begin with Jason; she hadn't even managed to attend to her bruises or change her soiled clothing from the incident at the warehouse earlier.

Her eyes scanned through the expensive things that Jason had in his ocean-view apartment, and she began to question how all his wealth was truly made. She had been in a relationship with him for almost four years now and would never have suspected him of doing anything illegal.

Until now.

The turn of the doorknob startled Julia, snapping her out of a scary thought that had just started to form in the back of her mind.

'I'm sorry about the warehouse. We're going out for dinner at Rob's, so go get ready.'

'I'm not going anywhere. Why did you hit me, Jason?'

'You stepped out of line. I can't have Gus seeing I can't even control my own woman.'

'Jason, do you hear yourself?'

'You shouldn't ask about things that don't concern you. I am paying you good money to work for me. Good enough for you to keep your damn mouth shut!'

'So that's what this is all about? You get me to work for you so that I keep quiet about what happens at the warehouse ...'

Jason swiftly approached Julia as if she had once again brought up a topic she wasn't meant to talk about. Julia had never felt fear of that level with Jason, but all his abusive language and forceful way of talking to her over the years had now started to take a physical form.

Julia once again felt the power of his forceful hands, lifting her from the couch by her arm, dragging her to the shower and pushing her in.

'You're hurting me, let go!'

'Go get ready, and that's final!' said Jason as he released his grip on her.

Jason left the bathroom and she locked the door behind him. Shaking violently from head to toe, she removed her clothes. Without waiting for the water to heat up, she stepped into the shower, drenched in fear even before the water had touched her body. She knew this was the point where she would need to end her relationship with Jason.

Saying it at the dinner table in front of Rob would be the worst possible time, given how concerned Jason was with her behaviour in front of people he knew. The cold shower woke her up to her true strength and clarity. She knew what she had to do and when. As she stepped out of the shower, she realised she was calm. She embraced the silence in the bathroom and smiled as a plan formed in her head.

As she selected a dress for dinner, her eyes found the suitcase tucked neatly in the corner of the closet. She had come to Marigua with only one suitcase; she needed only one to leave the island. As she slid into her dress, she heard Jason ending a conversation with Rob over the telephone.

'Are you ready or what? I'm not going to have Rob waiting for me all night.'

Julia stepped out of their room, ready to head out for dinner and ready to leave Jason forever.

CHAPTER 15

Jason had a pressing matter that he wanted to discuss with Rob but he had no intention of bringing it up in front of Julia. The only reason he'd brought Julia along for dinner was to keep up appearances and reassure everyone that he and Julia were fine after the incident at the warehouse. Jason was well aware of how word got around in his circle and was not prepared to show any sign of weakness.

Jason offered simple pleasantries during dinner, not expecting Julia to provide anything other than the usual formalities. Once they had finished eating and the plates had been cleared, he finally addressed her. 'I need to speak to Rob alone on some business matters. You can go home if you want to.'

He eyed Julia as she stood up from the table and left without saying a word. He could sense Rob was getting ready to ask him the burning question of the night but waited until Julia had long left the table.

'Does she know anything?'

'Of course not!'

'I heard from Gus what happened at the warehouse. That's not good.'

'You want to give me relationship advice now? I sorted it out. She'll never ask again.'

'The chief of police has been suspicious of us.'

'I know. Maybe some people need to disappear from this island.'

'No Jason, this is the chief of police we're talking about.'

'Wouldn't be the first time we had to make someone disappear.'

Jason looked at Rob, awaiting a response. He had an ice-cold look in his eyes.

'There's got to be a way around this.'

'I have my guy working at the station, but things are kept pretty tight with this new chief. The chief is working closely with the Boston police department and they are watching us closely. That much I know, from my guy.'

'It'd be better if the last chief was still around. Too bad he didn't look after his liver!' said Rob, laughing.

'You think this is funny? You want to know what it's like looking at steel bars for the rest of your life?'

'Jason, I know what you mean, but this is the chief we're talking about. Gus might want us to take a different approach.'

'Well, Gus will need to make an exception if we're going to continue doing business with him. I'll speak to him.'

Jason quickly stood up and left the table.

CHAPTER 16

Julia moved into a small cottage her friend Monica owned and rented out. It was thirty minutes away from the hustle and bustle of the port, but more importantly, it was at the opposite side of the island to where Jason lived. Julia felt fortunate that Monica had allowed her to rent her place for a couple of months while she sorted things out, especially given that Monica's husband, Derrick, a wealthy restaurateur, did not want his wife to get involved. Like most business owners on Marigua, he knew Jason's reputation only too well. Julia would only be on the island for a couple of months to enjoy island life without Jason and to get her affairs in order then she would be heading straight to Boston. She had already purchased her ticket.

In her years of being on the island, Julia had come to know Monica as a trusted friend—not to mention the only person that she was allowed to see without Jason present. She couldn't comprehend how she'd been on the island for so many years and only been allowed to see one person. Although Jason had never openly forbidden her from seeing other people or going places without him, he had certainly made it difficult for her to expand her horizons, always using excuses like *I don't trust other people* or *It's too dangerous for you to go there.*

She remembered going to the restaurant owned by Monica's husband to celebrate her birthday three years ago. Monica, who helped Derrick out from time to time, had happened to be there on that night. Monica had complimented Julia on how beautiful she looked in her dress. They got talking throughout the night and felt an instant connection—both women were from America and their partners were doing business in Marigua. They had exchanged telephone numbers and had been friends ever since.

She smiled to herself as the telephone rang.

'Hey Julia, everything alright at the cottage?'

'Everything's great. The place is so nice and cosy. Love the backyard—the little trees.'

'That's great! Hey, I was meant to call you. It's about Jason.'

There was a momentary silence as Julia felt struck by that name again; she didn't want to hear it anymore.

'Did he cause any trouble at the restaurant?'

'No, he just wanted to know that you are alright. He knows now that you're living in the cottage.'

'Monica, why did you tell him? He wasn't supposed to know.'

'He said he wasn't going to cause any trouble, he just wanted to know where you were and if you're okay.'

Julia held back her frustration, reminding herself of the gratitude she had felt only minutes earlier.

'Well, he knows now. Anyways, are you free for dinner tonight? We could have some nice food and wine. I'll come by the restaurant.'

'Not tonight. Derrick and I already have plans—we'll not be in town.'

Julia felt disappointed. She really needed someone to talk to. She felt lonely and upset; she had never imagined that this was where she would be at thirty.

'That's okay, I'll have dinner here on my own.'

'Hey, how about this: come by the restaurant and have your dinner. I'll get one of our waiters to look after you.'

'I'm not sure Monica ...'

'I can't make it for dinner, but can I at least compensate?' said Monica. Julia could hear her smile on the other end of the phone.

'Alright then. But we've got to do dinner soon, okay?' said Julia chirpily.

As they ended the call, Julia jumped. Someone was at the door.

CHAPTER 17

Julia stood, cold and fearful, as her brain processed the familiar figure that stood outside. She was determined not to let Jason have his way; she had put up with years of emotional and verbal abuse, and now physical abuse as well. The incident at the warehouse had been her final sign that her relationship with Jason was not what she wanted, and she wasn't going to go back to him, regardless of his intimidating behaviour. Taking a deep breath, she opened the door a crack, just enough to see his face.

'What are you doing here, Jason?' she demanded finally, trying to keep her voice from wavering.

He smiled a little and cocked his head to one side. 'What are you doing here? Come back home, Julia,' he said gently.

'It's over, Jason. Just leave!'

As if by the flick of a switch, Jason's smile disappeared, and his face twisted in anger. Julia felt a powerful push from the other side of the door. She desperately tried to close it, but she was unable to overcome his brute strength. Eventually, she realised that fighting was futile and the door swung wide open. She knew she had to talk to him to make him go away.

'I just want you to come back! Isn't a week enough for you to clear that head of yours?'

'*What?* Who do you think you are, Jason?'

'Hey, listen up! You don't leave me! I leave you! I'll tell you when it's over!'

Julia felt an enormous fear overpower her, realising that her problems with Jason were far from over. She mustered up all the courage she had in her to overcome the dark forces right on her doorstep.

'Leave, or I'll call the police,' she said, steady and firm.

Julia saw Jason calm down almost immediately. The sword had struck and he looked like a wounded animal. He backed off from the door, staring long and hard at her before leaving angrily.

Julia had an uncomfortable feeling that this would not be the last confrontation she would have with Jason. However, she took comfort in the thought that she was going to leave Marigua for good—not because she was afraid of Jason but because she wanted to. She quickly wiped away a tear that had fallen onto her cheek. She was determined to leave as a strong woman.

She went into her room and looked through all of the outfits in her closet. She knew she was going to be having dinner on her own in Marigua for the first time. She picked up her best dress, held it in front of her and smiled to herself.

CHAPTER 18

The waves of Marigua crashed violently against the port rocks. Pete felt strands of Julia's hair stroking his face as they danced in the strong sea breeze. He noticed that her eyes were fixated on the horizon, deep in thought. From their vantage point on the high rocks of the port, they could see the power of each wave as it crashed against the rocks below. The full moon sat high and proud in the skies above, illuminating the waters of Marigua.

'These waves are so strong that they might take over this whole island one day, I tell you,' said Julia as she took a sip from the bottle of wine.

'Marigua has had heavy floods for years. I don't think this whole island will sink just because of a few strong waves,' said Pete with a laugh, hoping the humour might relax Julia, but she didn't seem to be in the mood.

She looked like she wanted to tell him something but didn't know how to go about it; her face seemed worried and tense.

'That's why I want to leave Marigua—because these waves will drown this island one day. I always had this feeling of being unsafe here.'

'Did Jason ever hurt you?' he asked.

There was a pause that loomed uncomfortably in the air while Pete waited for an answer. He turned to look at her, hoping for a response. She continued to stare coldly into the horizon, wondering where—or even *how*—to start talking about Jason.

'He would shout and raise his voice if I acted in a way that was not to his liking. I refused to be his puppet partner. It was a loveless relationship. All I was to him was a trophy. I thought he loved me, but I was wrong. I had had enough of his threats and living in fear.'

'Julia, did he ever hurt you?'

'Yes, he did hit me once.'

'How dare he!' Immediately, he pictured himself tracking Jason down and throttling him.

As if reading his mind, Julia's expression turned from anger to fear. 'Pete, Jason is a dangerous man and I don't want anything to happen to you.'

'He can't hurt us Julia. I'm here with you.'

Julia's eyes were filled with hurt and pain.

'Maybe this place changed him. I don't know. But after four years, I woke up one day and asked myself, *Who is the real Jason*, and I didn't like what the true answer was.'

Pete remained silent. He was glad Julia was with him as he truly cared for her.

'I still remember that morning when I woke up to tell Jason it was over. He was cutting fruit with a kitchen knife and he had this look of disbelief when I said I was leaving him. He pointed the knife at me and shouted at me, saying I would never survive without him. I walked into my room, gathered my packed suitcase, and as I was about to leave, I said goodbye and closed the door behind me. I heard him shouting through that closed door, saying *Let's see how long you last without me! Go back to being a waitress then!*

Pete wondered how she had endured the last four years. She seemed strong yet vulnerable and he had a sudden urge to whisk her away—far away, where Jason would never find them.

'But here I am!' Julia said suddenly, a smile of satisfaction spread across her face.

'I'm glad you left Jason and that we're together,' said Pete as he pulled Julia close to him and gave her a kiss on her cheek.

'It feels so right with you, Pete. I feel so loved and safe with you.'

'I'll always love and protect you.'

'Just be careful of Jason. He has some powerful friends on this island. I don't want anything bad to happen.'

'Don't worry. It's only a week till we leave for America. Everything will be fine.'

'I can't wait for us to start our life together. I feel like I want to leave right now,' said Julia.

'We'll leave this island together soon. Don't worry about a thing.'

'I love you Pete! I always want us to be together.'

Pete embraced her tightly. The moonlight smiled upon them, illuminating them in the dark of the night.

Pete whispered, 'I love you, Julia.'

CHAPTER 19

1981

Pete felt a warm whisper upon his ear. Gentle fingers ran along the side of his face, willing him to wake up.

'I love you,' said Marie.

Pete slowly opened his eyes to a warm morning. Rays of sunlight painted a light orange canvas across Pete's bedroom wall. He wondered for a split moment if he was waking up from the night he had spent on the top of the port rocks in Marigua. It almost seemed like he was back in time with Julia in that instant, with the light orange rays softening his vision. He turned his head to the side and saw Marie, her face lit by a beautiful morning smile.

Pete felt Marie's warm lips and soft embrace. The deep love he felt for Marie made him want to just tell her everything that had happened in Marigua, but it was the very same love that he felt for her that prevented him from making that decision. He did not want to ruin the love bubble that he lived in with her, that had been built over ten years. He spent years blocking memories of Marigua until he felt the only way to resolve the feelings of guilt was to put it into words, in a novel.

Marie had mentioned to him on several occasions how she prided herself on the honesty of their relationship. However, he had kept this secret for such a long time that it could destroy the very foundations of their bond if it was brought up now. He couldn't do it when he first met Marie and he couldn't do it now.

'I love you too,' he said, and he truly meant it.

'You know how proud I am of you. Your final book has got the best reviews—better than any of your other books. What a way to finish up!'

Pete smiled at Marie. The nightmares he had had in writing his final book could not overshadow the joys of its success. Yet, he still felt cold and lonely, as though trapped in a dark place where the past haunted him. The final book had somehow made him feel even guiltier and he felt the burning temptation to tell Marie everything. The book could be a fictional novel to everyone else, but there were elements of truth. He desperately wanted to share those truths with Marie, but did not know where to start or if by doing so he could end his marriage.

'The last chapter ...'

There was a brief pause; it almost seemed like the moment that Pete was going to open up, but it quietly slipped away.

'What about the last chapter?' asked Marie as she pulled slightly away from Pete.

'It took a while, but I got there and I'm glad it's all over.'

The words just didn't seem to want to come out of Pete's mouth to start the conversation. He choked, as if by a natural instinct to hide the past. Pete could see that Marie was anticipating more, but he went silent.

'Did you know *The Boston Times* have called it the finest work of Pete O'Neill and a thriller not to be missed?'

Pete looked at Marie, who was truly overjoyed with his success. His best work, if only Marie knew, was pretty much based on a true story. Pete had changed some details and characters, but the sequence of events were largely what had actually happened on that island. He looked at Marie, who awaited some sort of positive response. He knew saying nothing at all again would truly concern her. But he didn't feel it was right somehow to punish his marriage for something that had affected him in the past. He didn't want to bring the past into his relationship and somehow ruin the love and happiness in his life.

'Thanks Marie. This book would not have been possible without you. You have been my rock.' Even as he said them, he knew the words sounded dismissive, like he was locking the door to a conversation he didn't want to have.

Marie embraced Pete. This embrace brought warmth and comfort to him. He did not want to lose her, and certainly not her love, which he cherished so much.

'I know the decision to stop writing and start teaching at the university would have been a difficult one, but look on the bright side—you get to do something different and inspire others who want to be writers as well,' she said with a reassuring smile.

Pete smiled back. 'You are such an amazing wife, you know that?'

Marie's face lit up and she said, 'That's the Pete we want to see at the ceremony. Let's get out of bed—we have a big day ahead.'

CHAPTER 20

The final book had already been written, but Pete was desperately waiting for some sort of closure. It was like he had expected the book to release him from the anxiety and guilt that had crippled him for so many years. The book launch awaited him and he was starting to feel anxious. Despite reassuring his wife with a smile, deep inside him a battle of emotions was taking place.

The Boston Art Gallery had a grand entrance. Fans occupied the front and managed to completely hide two golden poles that held a ribbon waiting to be cut. Several reporters, including those from *The Boston Times*, were waiting for Pete's arrival in anticipation.

As Pete got out of the car, a few fans rushed towards him to ask for his signature. Pete smiled and signed a few books before he had to politely move on and start the night. As he reached the entrance, he raised his hands to get the crowd's attention and said, 'Everybody, thank you so much for coming today and all your support throughout the years. Please join me as I cut the ribbon.'

Pete took the pair of scissors to cut the ribbon. His hands started to tremble. It might have been the overwhelming response of the fans present that had made him nervous, but Pete knew it was more than that. He felt like the emotions that he had been feeling for the past ten years were waiting to explode. A fan from the crowd shouted, 'Don't stop writing Pete. Love your books!' There was no response from Pete as he stood and stared at the ribbon. Pete looked towards Marie, whose eyes were concerned, demanding an answer. All these emotions were erupting just at the point of the opening ceremony, with a ribbon waiting to be cut and a truth waiting to be told.

CHAPTER 21

A huge explosion of applause erupted after the ribbon was cut. Pete could sense a wave of panic building up as he entered the function room. His mind was throwing itself into the scenes of his last chapter. The thoughts fired at him randomly and viciously. He could sense that Marie knew something was not right and he could no longer hold back the enormity of what had happened in Marigua. He was trying to think of how and when he was going to say it to her.

'Glass of wine, sir?' asked the waiter. Receiving no answer, he raised his eyebrows at Marie.

'Pete, would you like a glass of wine?' Marie repeated.

'Oh sure, thank you. I'm so sorry. Yes please, a glass of wine. I certainly need one.'

'Are you okay, Pete?'

Pete felt the sounds of the venue come to a standstill as Marie waited for an answer. He was desperately trying to swim back to the reality of what was taking place at the moment, but he knew he finally had to tell Marie what had happened in Marigua.

'Marie, I need to tell you something, but I can't do it in front of all these people. We'll leave soon and I'll ...'

'What's wrong Pete? Tell me.'

'We'll talk when we get back home.'

.....

Pete had to say goodbye to his fans halfway through, saying something had come up and he and Marie had to leave abruptly. He knew he could no longer stay; he had come to a decision finally to tell Marie what had happened in Marigua, and this time his resolve was firm.

As they walked out of the venue, Marie's hand gently stopped Pete from walking any further. Her pained eyes showed that she was ready to question him right then and there.

'Is there someone else in your life Pete?'

Pete looked at Marie. Her eyes had welled up with tears and he wondered how he was going to begin telling her about something that had tormented him for the last ten years. He didn't even know where to start.

However, the opening words seemed to just spill out from his mouth.

'Her name was Julia.'

CHAPTER 22

1971, 10 years ago

'This is our final night on the island, Pete. I can't wait to go back to America with you and start our life together!'

'I can't wait to start my life with you too, Julia.'

Pete embraced Julia like he never wanted to let her go. He had become greatly connected to her, despite it being such a short time, and the feelings he had for her were deep and unstoppable. Her smile brightened his life and her love filled his void with happiness.

'We must celebrate tonight!' said Julia excitedly.

'Yes, we should. What do you have in mind?'

'I'd like to go to Paolo's; we can have some food and wine there to celebrate!'

'Sounds perfect.'

The night was a perfect stage to set the scene for what

Pete believed was going to be a beautiful life with Julia. They were in love and their life together was about to start. All that was needed was to board the ship that was leaving Marigua the next day and due to arrive in Boston just a few hours later.

Meanwhile, unbeknownst to Pete, rumours had already spread that Julia was seeing a waiter who worked on the other side of the island, and what's more, they'd been spotted kissing in a restaurant that very night.

CHAPTER 23

Rob drove straight to the other side of the island to tell Jason what he had seen.

'Jason, I've got to tell you something! It's about Julia.'

Jason was sitting alone with his beer at his usual pub, deep in thought. He snapped out of his reverie when Rob mentioned Julia's name.

'Julia? What about her?'

'I saw Julia with someone. She was pretty intimate with him at Paolo's. Did you know about this?'

'Is this about some waiter guy that I've heard about? I knew there was a rumour going around that she was seeing someone, but I didn't know if it was true or not.'

'I saw it with my own eyes, Jason. She was kissing him in the restaurant.'

'You know, I gave her the whole world and this is what she does to me! Goes for some nobody waiter guy!'

'I'll get us a drink.'

Jason was fuming with anger as Rob signalled the waiter to bring two beers to the table. The waiter hurried back with the beers. Jason looked at the waiter and stopped Rob from paying. He was boiling with anger at the mere sight of the waiter and threw the money onto the floor.

'There you go! Just remember you're nothing but a waiter!'

The waiter hurriedly took the money off the ground and went back to the bar, afraid to spend another moment in the presence of the raging Jason.

The talking continued into the night; inevitably, so did the drinking.

'You know, Rob, she loves me and only me. Why would she go do something like that?'

'Jason, you need to fix this. You need to get her back. We can't have a waiter guy like that be seen with her. It leads to a bad reputation for guys like us—word is getting around that your expensive gifts and dinners aren't enough to keep your woman.'

There was a momentary cold silence. The sounds of people at the pub, and the waves crashing across the distant rocks, evaporated to nothing as Rob's words amplified in Jason's head. He drank the last of his beer, eyes bloodshot, and slammed the glass onto the table so hard that it startled Rob.

'I'm going to fix it!'

Jason's face was red with anger as he stood up and left the table abruptly, taking no further note of Rob, who yelled after him in vain.

Jason was in a different headspace. He walked across the street to his red Cadillac DeVille convertible and started it up in a hurry. His car roared out of sight as he headed to the other side of the island.

CHAPTER 24

Pete and Julia stumbled towards the door. Julia reached into her bag to get the keys but staggered before she could insert the key into the lock. They both burst out laughing.

'Am I that drunk?' said Julia, pausing to get the keys off the ground.

'You definitely are. Let me. I'm a little less drunk than you.'

Julia pulled Pete close to her after he had stood up. She paused and looked at him intensely.

'I love you Pete. I can't wait to go back with you.'

She pulled him closer and kissed him passionately.

'Let's go in and celebrate. Today is our last day on this island and we start our new lives tomorrow,' she said.

Julia got in the house and found herself opening another bottle of wine. Her happiness at leaving the island, together with the light-headed feeling from the wine she had been drinking, made her reluctant to stop the celebration.

'Julia ...' started Pete as he closed the door behind him and threw the keys onto the coffee table beside the couch. 'Maybe we should just relax,' he said, eyeing the bottle in her hand.

'What?'said Julia cheekily as she started filling up a glass of wine.

Pete smiled. 'Alright, alright. We'll have one more glass, then no more drinking for the night, okay?'

Julia nodded. She handed one glass to Pete and sat on the couch. 'Cheers to our new life and new beginning together!'

They sat back and talked long into the night. She enjoyed every moment of his company. In the bliss of their happiness, one glass of wine became several.

CHAPTER 25

Pete's eyes grew weaker and he became more exhausted as the night went on. The conversations seemed to slow down and the last thing Pete remembered was seeing Julia at the other end of the couch, about to fall asleep herself. His eyes began to shut and he mumbled his last words to her for the evening as she stood up.

'Julia ... Where are you going?'

.....

The alarm clock on the table started screaming. Pete jolted and found himself completely covered by a blanket. He must have set the alarm at some point in the night to make sure they woke up in time for their departure at noon. Pete stopped the alarm and checked the time. Nine o'clock. He moved the blanket and smiled, thinking of Julia's warm-hearted gesture.

The morning sun blinded him as he looked around for her. She was not on the couch. He couldn't see her in the kitchen either. He thought she might have been up earlier, preparing breakfast, but she wasn't. The house was silent. The only noise he could hear was the sound of crows cawing outside the house. Then came a strong gust of wind that made the rustling of dried fallen leaves in the backyard audible. Pete's head felt heavy from the drinking the night before.

'Julia?' he called.

The empty bottle of wine on the coffee table caught his attention. He realised that they had finished a full bottle. Hearing no response, he wondered if she had headed out for a walk. He wandered to the front door. Maybe she'd gone out for a quick stroll to sober up while he was asleep. He turned the knob and, to his surprise, it opened. The first rays of sunlight slowly crept in, warming his toes. He turned around and looked at the coffee table. The keys were in the exact same position they had been the night before. He then realised that the front door had not been locked all night. Suddenly, fearful and annoyed at his carelessness, he called out for Julia again.

'Julia!'

Still, no response.

He walked straight to the end of the kitchen where a small door opened to the backyard, thinking she might be sitting outside having a coffee. He turned the doorknob, but it was locked. Pete was confused. In a frantic moment, he unlocked the door.

It was silent, aside from the sound of rustling leaves against a slight wind. He turned around and locked the door once more. He took a deep breath and thought hard, trying to clear his mind. He felt a slight sense of relief as he realised that she may have moved to her bed. Yes, he remembered now—she'd been getting up just as he was nodding off. Smiling gently, he headed past the couch and walked towards the bedroom.

It seemed lifeless. Clearly, the windows had been shut, as there was no light illuminating the entrance. His smile fell immediately. It almost seemed like something unusual awaited him. Silence and gloom engulfed the entrance. His earlier relief was replaced by a strange sense of uneasiness. Something was amiss. Something just wasn't right.

CHAPTER 26

1981

Marie awaited Pete's confession. What was so wrong in their marriage that would prompt Pete to seek a relationship with someone else? Marie just couldn't put it together. There were no visible cracks that she knew of. She waited impatiently for Pete to say something more than just the person's name, now that they were in the privacy of their home, but he seemed at a loss for where to start.

'Some elements in my final novel were true. Chapter Thirteen was real.'

'What do you mean, Pete? I am so confused. What has this got to do with anything—with us?'

Marie thought about the last chapter. She knew he had struggled to write it, but still couldn't see how all of this was relevant—the woman in that last chapter had been murdered.

An uncomfortable thought popped into her mind.

'Did you do something wrong, Pete?'

Marie did not know what to expect. She had no idea how a night of celebration had turned into some sort of a breakdown in their marriage. Pete's hesitation made Marie even more fearful of what was going to be revealed.

'As you know, I worked as a waiter in Marigua and came back because things didn't work out there.'

'Yes. How is this related to the book and who is Julia? I'm so confused.'

'Something terrible happened on that island and I feel responsible for it.'

Marie's body began to shake with fear. Her mind was immediately flooded with bad thoughts. For a moment, she wondered if Pete had done something really bad and was about to confess it. She imagined the worst. She did not want to verbalise it, but the words came straight out her mouth anyway.

'Did you—'

'A woman was killed!'

And there it was. Marie couldn't believe what she was hearing. Pete was the most loving man she had known in her whole life. He was sensitive, kind and well-mannered; she could not comprehend how he could be capable of murder. An uncomfortable thought floated into her bubble of thoughts in that split second.

Pete had always been slow in talking about his life in Marigua. He had always shut down the topic of his life on the island whenever Marie brought it up. He often had an uncomfortable look on his face, and he would just simply say his life on the island hadn't worked out and it wasn't worth talking about.

Marie felt strangled by fear. Pete was about to confess the unthinkable to her. She didn't know if she wanted to stop him from speaking further or simply run out of the house. Her entire life was about to change. She had given him all the support he needed over the years and had been a loving wife, but what he had to say could change how she was going to feel about him for the rest of her life.

The air was still. The anticipation was so intense that it held Marie and Pete captive, their gazes locked onto one another. Marie waited for the deadly opening line.

'A woman was murdered. Her name was Julia and I was seeing her at that time.'

Marie's heart sank as the words came, piercing her heart like daggers, one after the other.

CHAPTER 27

1971, 10 years ago

Pete took his first steps towards Julia's bedroom. As he drew closer, his foot felt something strange. He looked down to see little drops of blood leading to her bedroom. He bent down and touched one of the red dots and looked at his finger. He became frantic and walked faster to her bedroom, noticing that the door was slightly ajar. He could see Julia's foot. She must be lying on the ground. His thoughts raced as he pushed the door open, unaware that he was opening a door to a world of miseries yet to come.

Pete's eyes fell upon a terrible sight that he never could have imagined waking up to that morning. Julia was lying on her back on the ground, motionless, with half her face bloodied. The left side of her skull was completely fractured. Splatters of blood were all over her bed sheets. The shirt and jeans that she had worn the night before were partially soaked in rivers of blood. Pete stood at the entrance of her bedroom, nailed to the ground. He was in a complete state of shock. He could not believe what he was seeing. Julia's dead cold eyes stared up at the ceiling.

Finally, he crossed the room and shook her lifeless body, shouting 'Julia! Julia!'

He cried out loud, wondering who could have done this to her. *What kind of animal could have killed such a beautiful soul?* The thoughts erupted from him. He looked around the room and his eyes found a scribbled note on the bedside table.

You can have your dead girlfriend now.

'Jason!' screamed Pete. He must be the one that killed her. He never got over Julia leaving him. Pete felt like murdering Jason in that instant. His eyes were bloodshot and filled with tears as he held Julia's dead body. He hugged her hard; the tears ran down his cheeks uncontrollably. He shouted for Julia to come back to him. His own clothing became stained with Julia's blood.

'Come back Julia! We're supposed to leave together! Wake up! Wake up!'

Filled with rage, he hurried to the kitchen and pulled out a sharp kitchen knife. He was going to confront and kill Jason for what he had done. He grabbed the knife and headed towards the door. Then suddenly, Julia's voice came to his head and he remembered her words about Jason. It was a moment that banished the impulsive thoughts that were driving him to kill Jason for what he had done and brought him back to reality.

He paused for a moment, sitting on the couch. He threw the knife onto the coffee table and buried his face in his hands. He was at the centre of a crime scene; everything would incriminate him, not Jason.

He mustered all his strength and forced himself to return to the bedroom, one foot in front of the other, one step at a time. When he reached the entrance, he fought the urge to vomit. He lifted her dead body and placed her gently on the bed. He then used a fresh blanket from the closet to cover her body. He knelt beside her bed like a person mourning at a funeral. His face rested gently on her chest as he hugged her waist. He wished his own body could warm hers to life.

'Julia! Wake up! We have a beautiful life waiting for us. We must leave together! Wake up!' said Pete as he hugged her, tears streaming down his face.

He held her, not letting her go, and the minutes of the clock flew past, one after the other.

A huge gust of wind beat violently against the entire house, shaking the windows. He heard what sounded like a knock on the front door. It startled Pete as he lifted his head from her chest, wondering who it could be. The thought of the police showing up at Julia's place and arresting him for her murder made his body turn cold. Pete stood up.

Then the loud knock at the front door came again.

CHAPTER 28

Pete waited for a moment, remaining completely still as the knocking continued. He did not know what to do, so he just held his breath, hoping whoever it was would go away.

Then he heard a female voice calling out, 'Julia? You there?'

Pete knew at that point that it was Monica; perhaps she had come by to say goodbye to Julia. Pete was aware that Julia had told only Monica that she was going to leave permanently for America. He remained still and made no sound or movement. He closed his eyes, clenched his fists and waited for the knocking to stop. He prayed to God that Monica would leave.

As he finished his prayer, a mighty gust of wind

started to build up, causing all the windows and doors in the house to vibrate violently. It was almost like a huge storm was about to break out on the island.

Then he heard a faint voice, partially drowned by the strong winds, saying, 'Oh my God, what weather is this?'

The violent wind continued for a while more and then the knocking stopped. Pete was certain Monica must have left. He looked at his bloodied clothes and then at Julia lying on her bed. His feet felt heavy, as if huge shackles had been placed around each ankle. Paralysed, he sat on the ground, not knowing what to do.

He wanted to hold Julia and be with her, but if he didn't let her go at this point, there was no telling what might happen to him, and there was nothing he could do for her now. He spotted his bag near her bed. He took off his bloodied clothes and changed into a fresh pair of jeans and a clean shirt. He made sure that the tickets were still in the bag—his ticket back home, to freedom. He looked at the tickets again and broke down in tears, coughing painfully as they got stronger. When he calmed down a little, he zipped the bag up once more.

He walked up to Julia's body and gave her a kiss on her lips. Tears rolled down his cheeks as he looked at her one last time before covering her face with the bedsheet.

He slung his bag over his shoulder and hurried out of the room. Before he closed the door behind him, he said,

'Goodbye Julia. I will always love you.' Tears streamed uncontrollably down his cheeks, blurring his vision. He wiped them away and headed to the front door.

As he slowly unlocked the door, he peeped through its small opening. There was no one around. He slid out of the house and looked around carefully to see if anyone was in the vicinity. There wasn't a soul around. Pete ran to the port for his freedom.

CHAPTER 29

Pete was breathing heavily, his heart beating fast from all the adrenaline and running. If he ran fast enough, he could reach the port just in time to board the ship. He could not afford to stop running; he knew if he missed the ship his whole life could be over.

Julia's voice suddenly came into his head. *I love you Pete! Keep running!* The tears threatened to return, but he controlled himself. He didn't want to draw any attention. As he stopped and caught valuable seconds of breath, he became aware that the pressure had built up so much that he could not hold it in any longer. He threw up on the side of a walkway. He could feel his ears ringing; he was seeing stars all around. It almost seemed like time had come to a standstill, and with the volume of the island fading away, the only sound he could hear was the ringing of his ears and his heavy breathing.

He paused for a moment as a gentleman walked up to him and asked him if he was alright. Pete quickly came back to his senses.

'I'm fine,' he said as he caught his breath.

'You sure?' asked the man.

'I'm fine. I'll be okay,' said Pete, patting the gentleman on his shoulder to reassure him that he was going to be alright.

'What time is it?'

'It's almost 11.30.'

Pete was not too far from the dock. He desperately needed to get to the ship. He thanked the gentleman for his concern and started to run again, his bag bouncing back and forth across his shoulders. He could see from a distance the last line of people boarding the ship. He ran as fast as he could, reaching the boarding gate just as it was about to close. He stopped behind the last person in line to catch his breath. A crew member closed off any further boarding by stringing a chain behind him.

Pete had made it just in time. He lowered his bag to unzip it, took out his ticket and presented it to the boarding officer. Pete felt the boarding officer's look alone could convict him of a crime he never committed. Pete tried his best to keep his composure. He felt nauseous and close to vomiting again but didn't want to be rejected entry or bring any further attention to himself.

'This is not your ticket. Where is your ticket?' demanded the boarding officer.

'What do you mean? That is my ticket,' said Pete, confused, as fear started to grip him. He wondered if his ticket had accidentally been left behind at the house.

The ticket officer handed him back the ticket and demanded again, 'This is not your ticket! Where is your ticket?'

Pete took the ticket back. It had Julia's name on it. He could not believe he had accidentally handed over Julia's ticket in the frenzy. He dropped his bag to the ground and hurriedly began searching. He handed his own ticket to the boarding officer.

The man looked at the slip of paper, stamped it and handed it back to Pete, who thanked him with relief and rushed towards the ramp.

'Wait!' the boarding officer said as Pete was about to reach the ship.

Pete's heart skipped a beat.

'Whose ticket was it that you gave me before?'

Pete's heart raced as he tried to come up with a quick answer. His head was shouting at him to say something, but his mouth was having trouble churning the words out. As seconds went by and his lack of reply hung dangerously in the air, Pete began to look more and more suspicious. Then he pulled himself together at last.

'Oh, that's my girlfriend's ticket. She's not coming with me. I'm going back to America alone.'

The officer looked at him, seemingly convinced, as Pete tried his best to maintain his composure. He felt numb waiting for an answer. There was complete silence all around him.

'Alright, you can go,' the boarding officer said finally.

As Pete took his first step forward, he felt a strong hand up against his chest.

'Forgetting something?' said the boarding officer, looking Pete straight in the eye.

Fear rushed into Pete's heart, and for a split second he wondered why he was being stopped.

The boarding officer pointed to a bag that had been left behind on the ground. Pete then realised he had left his bag on the ground and completely forgotten about it. He took a step back, picked up his bag and entered the ship as the boarding officer shook his head in disbelief.

He could not believe that he had finally made it. He headed straight to the top deck after he boarded; he wanted to be in full view of the island he was leaving and watch out for anything that was going on at the dock area. He was still fearful that the authorities would stop the ship from leaving, that Julia's death might have already been discovered.

As he stood on the top deck, he surveyed the island one last time. The ship sounded its horn and began to move. The island's clock tower struck twelve noon. The sounds of the chime became softer and softer as the ship moved further and further away from the dock. Tears streamed uncontrollably down Pete's face as he left the island, alone. There was no Julia by his side; all that remained of her were the unforgettable memories in his mind and the precious time he had spent with her.

The noon rays hit the ocean and threw sparkles of diamonds across its surface. As the clock was halfway through its chime, Pete pulled out Julia's ticket and looked at it one last time. A long nail of pain embedded itself into Pete's heart as he released her ticket into the ocean. The ticket floated in the wind until it finally hit the water and sank into its depths as the clock finished its final note.

CHAPTER 30

Less than an hour into Pete's journey back to Boston, a storm began to brew. The ocean was violently throwing the ship from left to right.

'We're going to die!' shouted the man next to Pete as he gripped hard onto his seat.

Everyone on the ship was told to vacate the deck; powerful waves smashed against the bow. The deck crew were desperately fixing one thing after another or shouting instructions to other crew members.

Pete certainly didn't want his life to end like this. He closed his eyes and told himself that he was going to make it through this, no matter what. He had lost his father to the war, his mother to old age and the woman he loved to murder, but there was a small ray of hope in his heart, encouraging him to live on. There seemed to be a light at the end of the tunnel, even with everything that had happened. The waves continued to beat against the ship, throwing it from side to side. People on board were screaming and shouting.

Pete prayed to God to get him back home safe. He promised to make something out of his life. He had lost everything, but he wanted to live on and remember the people he loved. The closeness to death was so imminent that the desire to live on, even after what had happened, struck him like a bolt of lightning.

The man beside Pete cried out in fear and held on tight to Pete's arm. 'We're going to die! My wife and children will never see me again!'

Pete mustered up his courage and looked at the man. 'What's your name?'

'What?' said the man, a little confused. After a few seconds, he processed Pete's question and took a deep breath. 'I'm John.'

'John, we're going to be fine. We're going to make it. You and I—and all of us on this ship—are going to make it.'

John nodded and reluctantly released his grip. His eyes were filled with fear, but the hope that Pete had given him had calmed him down to some extent. Pete maintained eye contact with the man and began making small talk to distract him as the deck lurched to and fro.

Finally, the ship seemed like it was starting to stabilise. The waves seemed to get calmer as they sailed further away from Marigua. Gradually, the ocean returned to calm.

'Thank you Pete,' said John with a shaky grin.

Pete smiled back. 'I told you we're going to be fine, John.'

As the ship continued to sail calmly towards Boston, Pete and John continued talking.

'So, what brought you to Marigua?'

'I came to start a new life in Marigua, but I am going back to Boston now,' said Pete with a sharp pain in his throat.

'I'm sorry it didn't work out for you in Marigua.'

Pete grimaced and looked at his hands. 'What about you?'

'I own an editing and publishing business. I went to Marigua to meet a writer.'

'I do a bit of writing myself in my free time, but I wouldn't call myself a writer.'

'What sort of stuff do you write?' enquired John.

'I write fiction. It's nothing really. You said you had a family, a wife and children?'

'Yes, I do. My wife Tracy and I have a three-year-old son named James. What about you?'

'I don't have any family. I'm on my own,' said Pete, sadness darkening his eyes.

John looked at Pete, sensing his sadness, and reached for a briefcase underneath his seat. 'That's my card,' said John as he pulled out his business card and handed it to Pete. 'You said you do a bit of writing. Come by my office and maybe we can talk a bit more about it.'

Pete was in complete shock. Even from that short interaction, Pete could sense that John was a pleasant person to be around.

At that moment, the horn sounded to let the people on board know they were about to reach Boston. People were clapping and shouting joyfully.

'I'm happy I can see my wife and son again Pete. Thank you.'

'I'm glad we're all home safe too.'

As the ship reached the dock, Pete wondered what his life in Boston was going to be like now that he was back. There was a moment of silence between John and him as they were leaving the ship.

John broke the silence. 'Pete, I really hope you will come by the office. You've got my card, right?'

'I've got your card. I will surely come by,' said Pete with a smile.

John shook Pete's hand and briefly returned his smile before both men went their separate ways.

CHAPTER 31

As Pete was about to exit the checkpoint at the port, he noticed the Boston police force was waiting close by. As he handed his passport to the checkpoint officer, his heart raced. His ordeal was far from over. It might be the beginning of a very painful journey.

The checkpoint officer looked at his passport and eyed him suspiciously.

'Pete O'Neill.'

'Yes, that's me.'

'Just wait here for a moment sir.'

Pete watched as the checkpoint officer got up from his seat and walked straight to the police. He knew it was all over. There was very little he could do to prove he was not responsible for the murder. All he could do was tell the truth and hope it would set him free. His mind was lost in thoughts of losing his freedom, possibly forever.

The world was suddenly in slow motion, although everything around him was happening at lightning speed. He saw, in a flash, a group of police officers rush towards him. Then a set of brutally cold handcuffs encircled his hands, making him wince. A loud voice barked *You have the right to remain silent* and the words paralysed him.

The police car drove off with Pete occupying the felon's seat. It whizzed past the buildings of Boston, and Pete thought that this might be his last view of the outside world. The police siren played its continuous loud rhythm, announcing his crime all the way from the port to the police station.

His ears were still ringing with the police sirens as a strongly built police officer sat him down in the interrogation room.

'I'm Officer Masarone,' the man said. 'Do you know why you're here, Pete?'

The policeman was muscly and clean-shaven, every bit the picture of authority. His uniform was pristine and looked freshly pressed. This was obviously a man who paid attention to the finer details. Every inch of his dark hair was combed in place and he had a dead cold look in his eyes. His voice was heavy and it echoed long after he had finished his sentence.

'I didn't do it.'

'I didn't say you did anything, so why are you denying anything?'

Pete finally found his voice, filled with anger and pain. It all erupted and spilled out; he was ready to wrestle with Masarone.

'I know why I'm here. It's because of a woman called Julia. Someone murdered her and I know who it is. It is an American businessman called Jason who lives on that island!'

Masarone leaned forward as if a familiar name had popped up.

'Did you say Jason? What do you know about this Jason guy?'

'He was Julia's ex-boyfriend and works at the port doing import-export. He killed her.'

Pete noticed Masarone was jotting down the words as if he had to quickly get a message across to someone.

'How do you know that for sure? Why didn't you go to the police? I'm curious that you chose to run away, yet you're saying you're innocent.'

'He left a note near her bed. I didn't go to the police 'cause he knows people and I would have been locked up in prison for the rest of my life for a murder I didn't commit.'

Pete couldn't understand why the name 'Jason' and

'living in Marigua' would have such an impact, but clearly it had.

'Okay, stay here. I'll be right back. We're not done yet.'

Pete saw Masarone leave the room, and as the door closed, he heard Masarone shout, 'Put the chief of police of Marigua on the phone, *now!*'

CHAPTER 32

Jason felt a loud bang. His head felt heavy and clouded from all the booze the night before. He winced as the banging continued.

'Alright, just wait!'

He got up from his couch and staggered past several cans of beer, his vision slightly blurred. He wiped his eyes as he approached the door. Desperately wanting to throw up, he willed the thumping on the door to stop. Feeling agitated, he walked faster and turned the door-knob, opening the door to unexpected visitors.

'What the ... ?'

A slight burst of reality hit Jason as he looked down to see himself still dressed in his bloodied clothes. In desperation, he tried to slam the door shut, but the police chief and two other officers prevented him. He struggled for a while, holding them off for as long as he could before he fell to the ground.

For the first time, Jason felt the hands of the law. His hands were viciously pulled behind his back and he felt the tight handcuffs snap shut, taking away his freedom of movement. As he lay on his side, he found himself face to face with a bloodied baseball bat. His time was up.

CHAPTER 33

1981

Marie felt angry and disappointed after Pete had finished telling her what had truly happened in Marigua. Every part of her wanted to believe what he had said, but she was still grappling with the fact that he had hidden the matter from her for ten years.

'If the island sank a few days after you got back, how do I know if everything you're telling me is true?'

'You can speak to the Boston police department. I was released a few hours after I was arrested because they caught Jason.'

Marie was still trying to put all the pieces together. Some fit and others needed more time. She was physically and emotionally drifting away from Pete.

She stood up from the couch and walked into their

room. A few minutes later, she came out with a suitcase full of her things and looked at Pete sadly.

'I need to be away from you for some time Pete.'

'Marie, where are you going? I told you everything.'

'Yes you did. After ten years!'

'I didn't want to hurt you.'

Marie continued walking to the front door and just before she closed the door behind her, she looked at Pete and with tears in her eyes said, 'But you have.'

CHAPTER 34

1971, 10 years ago

Pete stood in the street and read the newspaper headlines.

The Sinking of Marigua—Forces of Nature,
Climate Change or an Act of God?

It had been almost a week since Marigua had sunk, but it was still on the front page of every newspaper. The Atlantic Ocean had completely engulfed and buried the island three days after he had left. It would now be nothing more than a memory to everyone who had ever visited it.

Pete felt fortunate to be alive, but he didn't know how he was going to survive the painful memories.

They were all beginning to surface, like the debris of a destroyed ship.

As he sat on the park bench, he pondered his life. He remembered the words he'd said to himself when the ship had faced the storm. He'd promised himself that he would make something of his life.

Nevertheless, his painful memories had continued since he left Marigua. He felt guilty for leaving Julia behind in the state that she was. He resented not calling the police himself whilst he was on the island. He had, instead, fearfully run back home. He blamed himself for not locking the door, because if he had done so, Julia would still be alive. He felt angry at himself for not being sober enough to hear the front door open and protect her that night. In the back of his mind, he knew that Jason was responsible for the murder, but he loaded every other reason for her death onto himself.

Whilst battling with these emotions, he knew he had to do something with his life now that he was back in Boston. He pulled out his wallet and searched for the card John had given him. He carefully read every word on the card.

John Smith, Owner and Chief Editor,
Boston Publishing House

He paused and his thoughts ignited. He got up and rushed back to his cheap apartment.

He sat on his table and adjusted the table lamp. He took his pen and a piece of paper from the drawer and started writing. He wrote day and night for weeks until he was finally at John's office with a full manuscript in his hand.

CHAPTER 35

1981

Pete felt a gentle hand touch him on his shoulder as he woke up from the couch. He opened his eyes and saw Marie standing above him with a weak smile. He had not seen Marie for weeks; she had left to stay with her parents. Pete felt embarrassed by the several wine bottles near the couch.

'I'm sorry about all this. If I'd known, I would have cleared this up and shaved at least,' he said, gesturing to the mess with a sweep of his arm.

'I'm sorry I didn't answer any of your calls. I just needed some time.'

Pete wondered if this was the end of his marriage. It would be another fatal event in his life, with the people that he loved leaving him. He felt forsaken at that point. He had finally told her the story, but it was ten years too late.

He tried to comprehend why it had taken him so long to unleash the truth. He thought of all the times he had wanted to open up the conversation on what had happened but hadn't wanted to spoil the happiness of their marriage. He often thought it would be better for him to deal with it on his own; maybe, with time, it would all simply go away. He had certainly misled himself, thinking that writing his final book as a novel would set him free from the burden of Julia's tragic death.

'Follow me. I'd like to take you somewhere,' said Marie as she walked toward the front door.

She had an envelope guarded tightly in her hand. She smiled encouragingly at him, pressing the envelope against the side of her thigh. Pete could not imagine a life without Marie. He loved her dearly and his life would be so empty without her. He felt breathless at the thought of her leaving him forever. His throat tightened as he thought about what might be in that envelope. He wanted to say so much—how sorry he was for keeping a secret, that it had nothing to do with him not loving her—but instead he continued to endure the painful silence.

Pete stood up and walked towards Marie. They made what might be their final exit out of the house as a married couple. His eyes found their way to the envelope she was holding and she looked back at him as if she had only bad news for him.

'Let's go,' she said as she opened the door. There was hurt mixed with uncertainty in her voice.

Marie started walking ahead of Pete, deep in thought. Pete wondered where she was taking him. The questions filled his head. The strong morning winds blew hard against the envelope, which made disconcerting flapping sounds. There were no happy chirping birds, no smell of fresh flowers, just a beating cold morning wind. A fresh tear fell from Pete's eye as he realised Marie was heading to the port. The port was where Pete had proposed to Marie; maybe that was where she was going to end their marriage. His mind was racing. He wished he had told her everything sooner and hated himself for not doing so.

The morning skies above were almost an exact reflection of the dark-grey port waters. The cold winds had subsided and the air was empty, as if waiting to be filled with Marie's words. She walked toward the jetty. Each step toward the edge seemed like the final steps to an ending.

As they reached the end of the jetty, Marie turned and faced Pete.

'I spoke to Officer Masarone. He told me everything I needed to know.'

'Marie, I—'

'Do you love me, Pete?' she asked.

Pete answered without hesitation.

'I do, Marie, with all my heart.'

He found himself overcome with dread, knowing that she was about to say that she no longer loved him after this betrayal. His body was shaking in anticipation. He could see Marie's hand nervously tapping the envelope on the side of her leg.

'What about Julia?'

'I did love her … when we were together. But now it's only you, Marie.'

'If you love me, why did you keep this a secret from me for so many years?'

'I didn't want to hurt you. I thought I could deal with the hurt myself; I didn't want this tragedy to haunt you like it did me.'

A moment of silence lingered uncomfortably in the air. Marie was deep in thought.

'Marie, the anxiety I've been feeling for all these years was not just stress. It was me trying to cope with what had happened. I thought it would all go away someday.'

'I'm really hurt to know that after so many years of marriage you could not mention a single word about what happened in Marigua. You know I would have helped you with the pain.'

'Marie, none of this was meant to hurt you. I didn't know how to deal with it, and then I met you and the years went on and here we are. I kept the truth a secret to protect you! Or at least I thought it was protecting you; I didn't want to ruin what we had. I love you, Marie ...'

Marie stared deep into Pete's eyes before she threw her arms around him and hugged him tightly. The simple genuine words she heard from Pete had brought her back to him. They hugged each other tightly for over a minute without saying anything before Marie released him.

'There's something I would like you to do with me. Show me your hands,' said Marie.

Pete wasn't sure what to expect, but he held out his palms obediently. Marie started to open the envelope. She tipped half the contents into his hands and the rest into her own. Incense ashes. Sensing Pete's confusion, Marie began to explain.

'What happened to Julia was tragic, but it was no fault of yours. Let's both release these ashes into the water as a sign of peace towards her soul and hope it helps you find peace as well.'

Pete nodded his head in agreement, and they released the ashes into the port waters. Pete felt his body fill with peace. As the morning sun rose and threw its first rays across the port, the ashes dissolved gently into the water.

Pete finally felt free. He'd thought the last book would be the answer, but it was Marie's love that had truly enabled him to find the peace he had been looking for the past ten years.

EPILOGUE

Pete could feel the warmth of Marie's kisses on his cheek as he left home. The demons which had haunted him for years had finally left him. Pete had finally been able to move on with his life by coming to terms with his past. He would never forget Julia, but he also had to let go of the pain of what had happened to her. He only wished her soul could rest in peace. The unconditional love his wife had for him had not only saved his marriage, but also himself.

As Pete approached his destination, he felt ready. He felt blessed to have Marie in his life and he loved her with all his heart. The door was waiting for Pete to push it open. With contentment, happiness and love in his heart, he opened the door to a full auditorium.

'Good morning students.'